BOATS will FLOAT

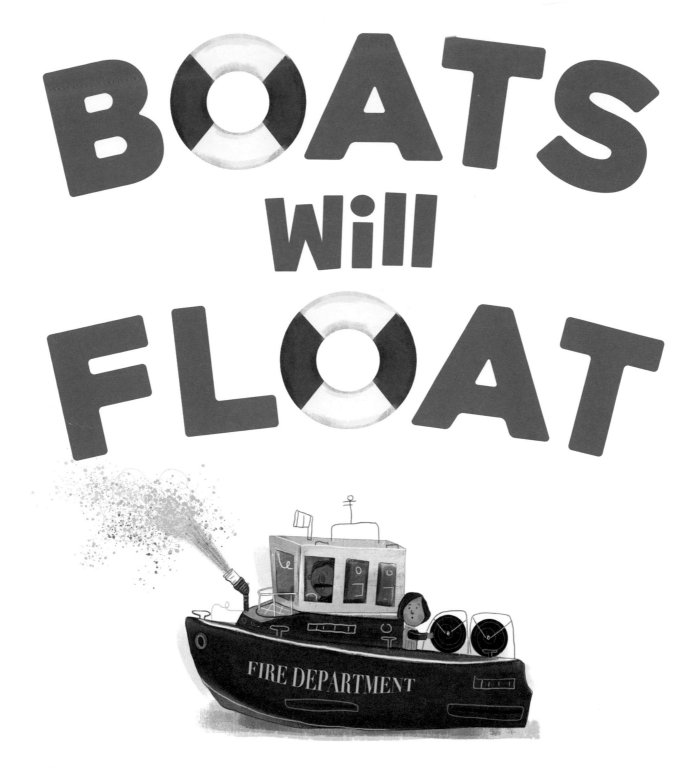

Andria Warmflash Rosenbaum • Illustrated by **Brett Curzon**

PUBLISHED BY SLEEPING BEAR PRESS

Boats are bobbing in the bay,
Waiting to be on their way.

Longing for the reaching tide.
Needing to explore and glide.

Early morning, rise and shine,
Fishing boats with nets and line.

Underneath a cloudless sky,
Dragon boats go flying by.

Motor purring.
Captain calling.

Salty breezes.
Seagulls squalling.

Boats will float into the ocean,
Rise and fall in liquid motion.

Sunlight sizzles, hot and bright,
Speedboat launches human kite.
Soaring up and sailing free,
Crystal spray and aqua sea.

Roller-coasting—
High and Low.

Boats will float
    through gales that *blow*.

Fireboats and tugs that lug,
Oogah-oogah-chug-chug-chug!
Scow and schooner, tanker too—
List of chores for busy crew.

FIRE DEPARTMENT

Coast guard, freighter, ships that cruise,
Offer front-row ocean views,
Leaving foamy, frothy trails,
Passing pods of spouting whales.

Research vessel underway,
Studies sea life day by day.
Divers visit ancient caves,
Coral reef below the waves.

Far below, a submarine,
Working hard to stay unseen,
Travels at a steady pace,
Housing sailors, short on space.

Whitecaps clapping,
Flags that flap,
Boats will float and never nap.

Trawler crawling near a bridge,
Steers around a rocky ridge.

Redbrick Lighthouse
standing tall,
Welcomes boats
both big and small.

Soft, warm breezes lull and lift.

Skipjack sails as currents drift.

Sunset melts in ocean's blue.

Moon comes in a curved canoe.

Houseboat floats and gently rocks,
Tied up tightly to the docks.
Anchored down upon the sound,
As milky moonlight skips around.

Sandy bottoms, sudsy tub,
Toy boats gurgle . . . **glub**, **glub**, **glub**.

Safely moored in dreams all night—
Boats will float . . . toward morning's light.

CANOE:
a slim, lightweight boat with pointed ends, driven by paddling

COAST GUARD:
a part of the United States Armed Forces that works to protect the American coasts, often performing rescue missions for boats in trouble

CRUISE SHIP:
a very large passenger ship that functions as a hotel and offers vacation activities

DRAGON BOAT:
a boat powered by many paddlers, often in special races. The dragon boat has its beginnings in China and has the head of a dragon at the front of the boat and a dragon tail at its back.

FIREBOAT:
a special boat equipped with nozzles and pumps made to fight boat fires and fires by the shoreline

FREIGHTER:
a large ship made to carry supplies, goods, or cargo

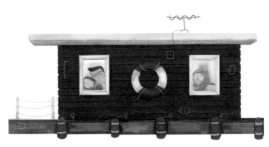

HOUSEBOAT:
a flat-bottomed boat fitted with a house on top of it and usually moored (fixed) to a dock so it won't float away

RESEARCH VESSEL:
a ship made to carry on scientific studies and explorations at sea

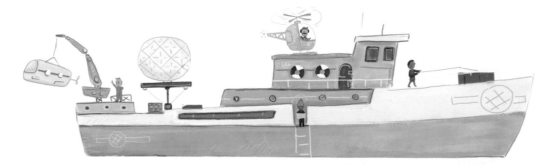

SCOW:
a large sailboat made with a flat hull and wide ends, used to carry bulky cargo

SKIPJACK:
a vertical-sided sailboat with a hull shaped like a V, often used to catch oysters

SPEEDBOAT:
a boat with a motor, often used for fun activities like fishing or waterskiing

TANKER:
a heavy-duty ship made to transport and hold large amounts of chemicals, oil, or gasses

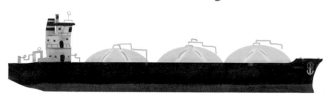

TRAWLER:
a type of fishing boat

TUGBOAT:
a small boat made to push or tow much larger boats in places where it's tricky for larger boats to move, such as in ports or near docks

SCHOONER:
a sailing ship with two or more masts (tall poles with sails) of different sizes

SUBMARINE:
a long tube-shaped warship equipped with torpedoes and sonar designed to operate underwater

For Natalie—agent extraordinaire times two!
—AWR

For Tracey
—BC

Sleeping Bear Press thanks Nathaniel Bacheller for his assistance
and careful review of the vessels in this book.

• • •

Text Copyright © 2020 Andria Warmflash Rosenbaum
Illustration Copyright © 2020 Brett Curzon
Design Copyright © 2020 Sleeping Bear Press
2395 South Huron Parkway, Suite 200, Ann Arbor, MI 48104
www.sleepingbearpress.com © Sleeping Bear Press

Printed and bound in the United States.
10 9 8 7 6 5 4 3 2 1

Library of Congress Cataloging-in-Publication Data
Names: Rosenbaum, Andria Warmflash, 1958- author. | Curzon, Brett, illustrator.
Title: Boats will float / written by Andria Warmflash Rosenbaum ; illustated by Brett Curzon.
Description: Ann Arbor, MI : Sleeping Bear Press, [2020] | Audience: Ages 4-8.
Summary: Illustrations and simple, rhyming text observe a wide
variety of boats that spend all day, from early morning until
dreamy night, on a bay, in the ocean, or under the sea.
Identifiers: LCCN 2019036852 | ISBN 9781534110410 (hardcover)
Subjects: CYAC: Stories in rhyme. | Boats and boating--Fiction.
Classification: LCC PZ7.R718726 Bo 2020 | DDC [E]--dc23
LC record available at https://lccn.loc.gov/2019036852